To my parents, who are the source of everything good that has come to my life.
Thank you for your unconditional love. To Alia and Walid, from whom I have learned
to keep my head up high, to love and to never give up. Thank you for showing me
the way. To Yazeed and Najd, you are our strength and our joy. Even in darkness, you
are the reason it has been possible to scream out loud. To every single person who
has shown me support: because of you, I believed I could do it.
To you, Loujain, my hero.— LINA

To all young girls who fight for their voice and rights—we are with you.
To Loujain, our hero. To Leela, always.— UMA

For little Nadi Luna, with love.— REBECCA

minedition

A division of Astra Publishing House
North American edition published 2022 by mineditionUS

Text copyright © 2022 by Uma Mishra-Newbery and Lina AlHathloul
Illustrations copyright © 2022 by Rebecca Green

ISBN: 978-1-66265-064-2
ISBN: 978-1-66265-077-2

First edition

10 9 8 7 6 5 4 3 2 1

mineditionUS
An imprint of Astra Books for Young Readers,
a division of Astra Publishing House
astrapublishinghouse.com
Printed at Grafiche AZ in Verona (BA), Italy

This book was illustrated in acrylic gouache and colored pencil,
and typeset in LoujainScript typeface. It was edited by Maria Russo,
Leonard Marcus, and Octavia Saenz, and designed by Nikolas
Brückmann. We also thank Annika Siems, Michael Neugebauer,
Deborah Sloan, Jessica Craig, Ben Schrank, Jack W. Perry,
Stephanie Ratzki, and Alisa Trager.

LOUJAIN
DREAMS OF
SUNFLOWERS

THE CARPET OF A MILLION SUNFLOWERS

WRITTEN BY
LINA ALHATHLOUL & UMA MISHRA-NEWBERY
ILLUSTRATED BY REBECCA GREEN

DO YOU BELIEVE YOU CAN FLY?

I KNOW I WILL FLY –
NOT IMMEDIATELY,
BUT DEFINITELY.

Every morning when Loujain woke up,
she squeezed her eyes shut and remembered
what she had dreamed the night before.

Loujain always dreamed of two things.
She dreamed she could fly.
And she dreamed she would fly to a place her baba
described as the carpet of a million sunflowers.

After getting out of bed,
Loujain followed her baba into the garden
and waited for him to open the door of the shed,
so she could catch sight of their wings.

First her baba would take
out his own wings.

Then he would hand
Loujain hers.

Loujain put on her wings
and ran around the garden,
pretending she could fly.

Once her baba's wings were on, he smiled at her, then leaped into the sky. Loujain watched as her baba soared, becoming smaller and smaller in the blue sky. She lifted her arms to the sky as her baba disappeared from view, wishing she could fly with him.

But because Loujain was a girl,
she was not allowed to fly.

On school days, Loujain walked to school with her brothers and sisters. She stopped to take pictures with her camera of any color she saw besides the gray of cement and the beige of sand.

She gave her baba her camera film, so that he could get
the pictures printed. Every week Loujain would add
the pictures to her ever-growing wall of colors.

In the center was a photo her baba had given her.
It was the most colorful one of all.

Often when she looked at it she would close her eyes and touch the picture, imagining she could feel each color in it — and even imagining she could hold each color in her hand. The brightest blue that was the sky. The deep green of the leaves and stems. The crown of yellow petals and the black seeds of each sunflower.

Floating in a sea of color,
Loujain felt free, as if she could do anything.

Loujain wondered if she would ever be able
to see the sunflowers with her own two eyes.
So at dinnertime she asked her baba
if she could go with him.

"Lulu" her baba said lovingly,
"the only way to see the sunflowers
is to fly over to where they are."

"But I don't know
how to fly, baba."

"One day, Lulu,
you will."

WHAT WONDERFUL NEWS!

At school Loujain told her friends that she, too, would fly someday.
But they called her silly and laughed at her.

In the courtyard,
her friend Ali tapped Loujain on the shoulder.

"You should stop telling people you are going to fly," he said.

"But Ali, one day I will! Don't you believe me?"

"You know that you can't, Loujain.
Girls are not allowed to fly," said Ali firmly.

Loujain gathered up her courage and said,

"You will get to fly.
I should be able to do the same!"

That day, Loujain rushed home
after school and ran to her room.
She threw herself down on the bed
and started to cry. But then Loujain
reached out to the sunflowers
on the wall.

"I will see you," she whispered.

The next morning
Loujain woke up early so that
she could talk to her baba.
"Baba, you must teach me how to fly now.
It is not fair that I cannot fly.
All the boys are already starting to learn.
Why not *me*?" Her baba looked at
Loujain for a long time.

Then he went
into the house.

Loujain's mama saw him come inside,
and asked him what was wrong.

"Lulu wants to fly," he said.
"But we both know she cannot, not really." Loujain's mama
thought for a moment. "Why should flying be only for boys,"
she said, "if we all can use wings?"

Loujain's baba listened. "If you don't support her, who will?"
her mama said. "You have to believe things will change.
Otherwise they never will." Loujain's baba looked at his wife,
then turned and went out to the garden.

After that day, Loujain always went out
just before sunrise to fly with her baba.
They watched together as the sky woke up with pink,
red, and gold. Loujain felt as if a color touched her skin.
She ran her fingers like a comb through the
awakening purple clouds and closed her eyes,
trying to memorize the feeling
of each color.

But at night Loujain would still dream of the sunflowers. One morning when it was very dark outside her baba woke her up.

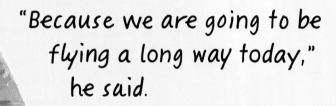

"Baba, why are we up so early?" Loujain asked.

"Because we are going to be flying a long way today," he said.

The house was quiet as Loujain and her baba slipped into the garden and put on their wings.

As they rose higher and higher
Loujain looked all around her.

The stars were still visible in the dark blue sky,
with a tiny line of orange on the horizon.

Loujain and her baba flew in silence.
With every flap of their wings
the sky awakened a bit more.

And then Loujain saw in the distance something that seemed strangely familiar: a sea of yellow and green.

She flew as fast as she could — she couldn't believe her eyes — it was the carpet of a million sunflowers!

Loujain landed in the middle of the field and stretched her arms straight up to the sky. At last! The brightest of blue that was the sky. The deep green of the leaves and stems. The crown of yellow petals and the black seeds of each sunflower.

Her baba took a picture of
Loujain flying above the sunflowers.

That night Loujain lay in bed, her eyes wide open.
She wondered if she would ever sleep again, now that she
had seen and felt and smelled every color from her dreams.

The next morning after their flying lesson
her baba and mama walked with Loujain
and her brothers and sisters to school.
As they passed through the market Loujain
noticed people pointing, whispering, and staring
at her, and she wondered what they were saying.
Baba stopped at a stand and bought a newspaper.

"Look, Lulu!" he said pointing at a picture.

It was Loujain. Flying above the field of sunflowers!
But then Loujain read the words around the picture.

She stared at the words uncertainly,
until her mama said,

"Lulu, we are proud
of you for flying."

As they continued walking through the market,
they passed the wing shop. There, a young girl was tugging
at her baba's shirt and pointing.

"Baba, Baba, teach me how to fly," she said.
"I want to see the sunflowers too!"

DO YOU BELIEVE YOU CAN FLY?

I KNOW YOU WILL FLY—
NOT IMMEDIATELY,
BUT DEFINITELY.

THE REAL LOUJAIN

A NOTE FROM LINA & UMA

Dear Friend,

When we wrote "Loujain Dreams of Sunflowers," Loujain AlHathloul — Lina's sister — was in prison in Saudi Arabia. Her crime? Speaking out for women's right to drive cars, something that men have been able to do for a long time.

Loujain's story and her voice continue to inspire us every day to dream and fight for a better world for all people. We hope this story does the same for you. Dream the impossible, speak bravely, and fly with the courage to make your dream a reality.

When we are young, sometimes we feel like the problems in our world are too big or scary for us to speak out to try to help fix them. And sometimes it feels impossible to dream of a world where we can speak out and be who we are meant to be — where we can fly. Loujain is our hero because she has always, from a very young age, fought for what she believed in. She reminds us every day that our dreams and voices matter, dear friends.

Do you believe you can fly?

We know you will fly — not immediately, but definitely.

ABOUT LOUJAIN ALHATHLOUL

Loujain AlHathloul is one of the leaders in the Saudi Women's Rights movement. With her friends and fellow activists, she worked to change laws in Saudi Arabia that made it illegal for women to drive cars, and even to work or travel without permission from male relatives who acted as their "guardians."

The first time Loujain was arrested was in 2013, when she moved from Canada, where she attended university, back to Saudi Arabia. She arrived in Riyadh and decided to drive home. Her baba filmed her driving, while he sat in the passenger seat. Loujain posted the video and it went viral.

Loujain was arrested for the fourth time on May 15, 2018 — just two months before the driving ban that she fought against was finally removed. She was brought to a prison where, for 35 days, she was not able to communicate with her family. All in all, she spent over two years in prison, without regular contact with her family. On December 28, 2020, Loujain was sentenced to five years and eight months in prison and labeled a terrorist and a traitor.

Loujain was released in February 2021 under strict constraints — she cannot leave Saudi Arabia for five years, she cannot continue her activism for three years, and she cannot speak publicly about her imprisonment or her release.

For her efforts to promote women's rights, Loujain has received many awards and has been nominated for the Nobel Peace Prize. In 2020, she was awarded the French Prix Liberte (French Freedom Prize) which is chosen by young people, ages 15 to 25.

Loujain now lives in Riyadh with her family, constrained under the terms of her sentence. She awaits the day when she can continue to fight for the freedom of all women and girls in Saudi Arabia and around the world.